Merry Christmas, Annie

Merry Christmas, Annie

written by Dana Bergman

based on the original novel by Thomas Meehan

PUFFIN BOOKS
An Imprint of Penguin Group (USA)

PUFFIN BOOKS
Published by the Penguin Group
Penguin Group (USA) LLC
375 Hudson Street
New York, New York 10014

USA * Canada * UK * Ireland * Australia
New Zealand * India * South Africa * China

penguin.com
A Penguin Random House Company

First published in the United States of America by Puffin Books,
an imprint of Penguin Young Readers Group, 2014

Library of Congress Cataloging-in-Publication Data is available.

ISBN 978-0-14-751360-1

Printed in the United States of America

1 3 5 7 9 10 8 6 4 2

Chapter One

When Annie escaped from the New York City orphanage in a bundle of dirty laundry, she didn't know how long she'd be gone. The orphanage had been her home for eleven years, and though she loved the other girls there very much, Annie couldn't waste another day in dreaming. Her parents had left her in a basket on the orphanage stairs when she was just a tiny baby, with a note promising to come back for her one day. But that day hadn't come yet, and

Annie couldn't wait any longer. She had to go find them herself.

For a while, Annie stayed with a couple named Fred and Gert Bixby, who owned a small pub on the Upper East Side. In exchange for food and shelter, Annie worked as a waitress and soon became a favorite among the customers. It wasn't easy, and Annie had to work very hard to earn her keep. She soon realized she'd never find her parents by settling in one place. And so, Annie ran away again.

But this time, she had nowhere to go, and winter was on the way. With only her dog, Sandy, whom she had teamed up with after leaving the orphanage, and a shabby, thin sweater to keep her warm, Annie set off downtown, toward Grand Central Terminal, a transportation hub in the center of Manhattan. Thousands of people walked through the station each day. Surely, Annie thought, she was bound to find someone who knew her mother and father.

But it seemed no one had time for a little girl. Everyone had somewhere to go, and all of the people were rushing to get there as if their lives depended on it. After a short while, Annie found herself walking toward a man selling apples by the Lexington Avenue entrance. He was a worn-down, bearded man in shabby clothes, but he had kind eyes. "Apples, apples! Shiny, red apples! Two for a dime! One for a nickel!" he shouted.

Annie stood a few steps away from the man, watching. What she would do for one of those big, shiny apples right now! Her stomach grumbled, and she heard Sandy's do the same. When the man noticed, he whistled for them to come closer.

"You hungry, little miss?" he asked.

Annie looked down, embarrassed. "Well, I . . ."

"Sure you are, we all are," the man responded. In 1933, the entire country was in the middle of what was called the Great Depression. Many people had lost their jobs and all their money. Some had even lost their homes.

The man handed Annie two round apples. "Here ya go, one for you and one for your dog. On the house."

"Gee, thanks, mister!" she said. It wasn't much, but Annie hadn't eaten since the day before, so it tasted especially delicious. She fed one of the apples to Sandy, who wolfed it down in two bites.

It was nearing the end of the day, and still, Annie and Sandy hadn't found a place to stay. Annie thought perhaps they'd sleep right there in the station. But then she spotted a group of police officers shooing the homeless men and women out onto the cold city streets and thought better of it. Instead, she decided to follow the apple seller to wherever it was he called home.

It turned out the man lived in what was called

a shantytown: a group of makeshift shelters built from wood and rusty scraps of metal. During the Depression, people who found themselves without homes gathered together to form their own communities. This particular shantytown was located under the Fifty-ninth Street Bridge along the East River, and Annie thought it was the perfect place for her and Sandy to stay the night.

"Come on, Sandy. I bet if we're lucky, these people will let us stay with them. And it looks like they're cooking something, too!"

They made their way down the hill toward a group of people huddled around an open trash can, warming their hands at the fire crackling inside it.

"Pardon me, folks," Annie said nervously. "But did anyone here leave a red-headed girl named Annie at an orphanage about eleven years ago?"

The men and women only shook their heads

or shrugged. But a kindly middle-aged lady looked up from the pot she was stirring and smiled. "You hungry, kid?" she asked.

Annie nodded, and Sandy barked happily. The woman passed around warm bowls of watery stew. It wasn't the best thing Annie had ever tasted, but it was better than the slop Miss Hannigan served at the orphanage.

"I'm Sophie, by the way," the woman said.

"My name's Annie," Annie said sheepishly.

"Pleasure to meet you, Annie. You got a place to stay tonight?"

"Uh, well . . ." Annie started. "I sort of ran away from the orphanage downtown. I'm trying to find my parents—they're out there somewhere, I just know it!"

Sophie gave Annie a knowing smile. "I bet they are, kid. But, uh . . . in the meantime, you could stay here, if ya like."

"Oh, gee. Could we? I mean, you wouldn't mind if—"

"Not at all. I've got just enough room for the two of ya," Sophie replied.

Only a few hours ago, Annie could never have guessed she'd find such friendly people to take her in. "What'd I tell ya, Sandy," Annie whispered. "A good meal *and* a place to stay."

Sophie helped Annie create a makeshift bed on the floor inside her small tin hut. There was barely room enough for one person, but they did what they could. Annie sat down next to her shaggy companion. Sophie was beginning to tiptoe out the door when Annie turned her head and said, "Gee, Sophie. Thanks for letting us stay with you."

"Don't mention it." She smiled a friendly smile before leaving the girl and her pup to themselves.

Annie snuggled up next to Sandy. Things were already looking up. *Maybe the sun will come out tomorrow*, Annie thought as she melted into sleep.

Chapter Two

Annie awoke the next morning to the bustling sounds of the shantytown. It was early, but Annie was used to being up before the sun. At the orphanage, Miss Hannigan woke the girls at the crack of dawn to start on their chores, and refused to feed them breakfast until they were done. But now, outside the hut, Annie could smell something cooking and the sound of Sophie's voice.

"Poor kid still thinks her parents are out there somewhere."

"All I can say is, that orphanage she came from had to be pretty bad for her to wind up here," said a man. Annie recognized the voice—the scruffy old man selling apples at the train station, the one she had followed here.

"Well, the least we can do is let her stay. No home. No parents. Right now, I reckon we're all she has," Sophie said sadly.

Annie stuck her head outside the hut and slowly walked over to where the rest of them stood. Sandy padded along at her side.

"Say, kid . . ." the apple seller said to Annie, "how would you like to come back to the station with me to sell these here apples? I'll bet we'll get twice as many customers with a little girl. All you gotta do is look sad and hungry."

"That won't be so hard." Annie shrugged. Hungry? Well, she was always hungry. But if Annie was anything, it wasn't sad. She always looked on the bright side. When the girls at the orphanage were down, Annie was the first one to cheer them up. Even when it came to finding her parents, Annie was full of hope.

"But with all due respect, mister, I'm trying to find my folks. And, well, I was thinkin', if I could save enough, I'd take the bus down to Florida. . . ."

"Tell ya what. You come sell apples with me, and we can split the profits. How does that sound? Then you can use the money to go wherever you'd like."

"Gee, really? You'd do that?"

"I ain't sayin' it'll be easy. It's hard work and long hours. But I bet one day you'll have enough money to get outta here."

Annie beamed. Finally she was on her way to finding her parents.

The apple seller—his name, Annie learned, was Randy—led the way to Grand Central Terminal. Both the man and the girl carried large baskets hanging from their necks, filled with rosy-red apples, while Sandy trotted along behind them. Annie was eager to be heading back to the station. Selling apples with Randy would earn her some money, but spending all day in the middle of Manhattan meant she was likely to find someone who knew her mom and dad.

Randy set his apples down by the Lexington Avenue entrance as always, and Annie did the same. Station-goers hustled by them. "Apples! Get your fresh, red apples! One for a nickel! Two for a dime!" they cried.

"Remember, an apple a day keeps the doctor away!" Annie added.

By the end of the day, Annie was worn out. But she and Randy had sold a total of forty apples. More than Randy had ever sold in a day's work.

"You did good, kid," Randy said, patting Annie on the shoulder. He handed her a fistful of coins—her share of the profit. It was more money than Annie had seen in her entire life.

"Leapin' lizards!" she said, her eyes widening at the sight.

"All thanks to you, Annie. We're gonna be rich!" Randy bellowed.

Annie accompanied Randy every day for the next three months. Together, they sold loads of apples, and Annie was able to save up almost enough for a bus ticket for her and Sandy.

One morning, on a particularly busy day at the station, Randy and Annie stood by the entrance doors with their bushels of apples. It was a day like any other, until Randy noticed a police officer heading their way. He didn't want any trouble.

"Quick, Annie," he whispered into her ear, "don't look now, but there's an officer making his way over. You need to get outta here, fast. If you ran away from the city orphanage, chances are someone's looking to get you back there."

Annie glanced up, and sure enough, a tall, ugly-looking man in a sergeant's uniform loomed closer. Before he could take another step, Annie grabbed Sandy's collar and started in the other direction. She didn't run, just walked very quickly so as not to draw attention to herself. After all, there were thousands of others rushing through the station; she would look just like everyone else.

But the officer knew who she was immediately. From her curly red hair to her tattered clothes, this was the missing girl from the orphanage. Annie kept her head down and moved along with Sandy, but the sergeant caught up and pulled her shoulder from behind.

"Excuse me, miss. I think I saw your picture in the newspaper. You're that runaway orphan."

Annie stood frozen. *Okay, calm down*, she told herself. *You'll think of something.* She managed to get a peek at his shiny gold name tag. It read *Ward*. "Uh, no, sir. I'm just here with my parents. They're right over there, see?" Annie pointed to a young couple waiting for their train to be called.

The policeman looked up, turning his head from side to side, trying to see over the mass of people. "Where did you say they were?"

But when he looked back down, to his surprise, the girl and her dog were gone, swallowed up by the crowd.

"Boy, that was a close one, huh, Sandy? We nearly got snatched by that officer!"

Sandy barked in agreement.

It was too dangerous to stay at the station, so Annie and Sandy made their way back to the shantytown. They would be safer there with Sophie and the other shanty folk. Of course, Randy would still be selling apples until late that night, wondering if Annie had gotten away. But once he came home, he'd discover that Annie and Sandy were okay after all.

Annie's relief only lasted for a short while. She didn't return to Grand Central Terminal again the next day, afraid Sergeant Ward would be back, waiting to catch sight of her and Sandy. What she couldn't have guessed, though, is that Sergeant Ward would find her anyway.

"Warm stew, Annie?" Sophie asked later that evening, ladling bowls of steaming soup and passing them around.

Annie shook her head. "No thanks, Sophie. I'm not feeling very hungry."

"What's got you down, Annie? You've been acting funny all day."

But before Annie could respond, they heard the sound of whistles blowing up the hill, followed by the glow of two flashlights. Police officers.

Stay calm, Annie thought. *They ain't here for you.*

The officers approached. "Okay, folks. Everybody outta here."

"What seems to be the problem, officer . . . Ward?" Sophie asked, peering at his name tag.

"That's *Sergeant* Ward, ma'am. And we got a court order to tear this place down. Causing a health hazard, or something."

"But we ain't hurtin' nobody down here. We got no place else to stay!" Sophie panicked.

"Sorry, that's the order. Now pack up and get on outta here."

Nobody seemed to notice Annie there in the dark. But then a flashlight shined in her face, and her eyes squinted shut automatically. "Hey, you!" Ward shouted. "You're that orphan with the dog. The one who got away!"

"Oh, no, sir," Annie said innocently. She pointed to Sophie. "I'm her daughter."

Sophie nodded, but Sergeant Ward wouldn't be fooled twice. He grabbed Annie by the shirt collar.

"You're comin' with me," he rumbled as he turned Annie around to face him. He had horrible breath and wore an evil grin on his face. "And your little mutt here is goin' straight to the pound."

Annie swallowed hard. She knew she'd have to accept her fate, but that didn't mean Sandy had to suffer, too. "Run, Sandy!" she yelled. "Run away, boy!"

Sandy whined softly. He didn't want to leave Annie, but he knew he couldn't stay. Swiftly, he took off into the night before either of the cops could stop him.

A tear came to Annie's eye. Would she ever see Sandy again? It hurt too much to think about.

"Back to the orphanage for you." Sergeant Ward chuckled as he dragged Annie up the hill. Annie looked back one last time at Randy, Sophie, and the other shanty folk who had been so kind to her these last few months. She shrugged her shoulders as if to say, *Well, this is it, I guess.*

The group looked miserable. Over the months, Annie had become part of their family, and they were sorry to see her go. But there was nothing they could do to stop it.

Chapter Three

Later that night, a knock came at the door of the New York City downtown orphanage.

"Yeah, who is it?" Miss Hannigan called out. She sat at her desk in a frayed silk bathrobe, listening to her favorite show on the radio. Her frizzy hair was tossed up in a messy bun, and her makeup was smeared down her wrinkled face. Clearly she wasn't happy about the unexpected disturbance.

"Sergeant Ward from the Seventeenth

Precinct. We found your runaway," the sergeant said from behind the closed door.

Miss Hannigan's eyes widened. "That little rat Annie," she mumbled under her breath, as she got up, primping her hair and retying her robe.

She threw open the door. "Well, well, well, if it isn't my dear little Annie come home," said Miss Hannigan sweetly. "Thank you, officer. Wherever did you find her?"

"She was living with some bums by the East River in one of those shantytowns."

"They weren't bums," Annie said under her breath, arms crossed.

"She had some mangy mutt with her, too. He got away, but we'll find him and slap him in the dog pound."

"I bet you will," Miss Hannigan said, gripping Annie's arm tightly. Annie squirmed.

Poor Sandy, Annie thought. Where was he

now? Hungry and homeless on the street with no one to take care of him. She let out a big sigh.

"Thank you again, Sergeant Ward," said Miss Hannigan, trying her best to remain calm. For all the grief Annie had caused her, Miss Hannigan couldn't wait to hand out punishment once the sergeant was gone.

Sergeant Ward tipped his hat. "All in a day's work, ma'am. And you," he said, glaring down at Annie, "don't ever let me hear that you ran away from this nice lady again."

It took all Annie's strength not to roll her eyes in the sergeant's face.

The instant the door closed, Miss Hannigan grabbed Annie by the scruff of her neck. "I'll have your head for this, missy." She dragged Annie into her office and slammed the door. "You'll be sorry you ever ran away after I'm done with you."

But before Miss Hannigan could lay another finger on Annie, the doorbell rang again.

"What is it this time?" Miss Hannigan moaned. She got up to answer the door.

A beautiful young woman stood in the doorway. She was dressed in the finest clothing from head to toe, her blond, hair tied back perfectly under a fancy pink hat.

"Miss Hannigan, is it?" she said. "Good evening, my name is Grace Farrell, and I was told by the New York City Board of Orphans that I—"

"Oh, of course! Come in, come in." Miss Hannigan nearly choked on her words.

The Board of Orphans had been sending representatives for random inspections of the orphanage and to check on the girls. Needless to say, both were suffering under Miss Hannigan's care. But Miss Hannigan was desperate not to lose her job. It was the only thing keeping her off the streets.

"And who is this young lady?" asked Grace, seeing Annie huddled in the corner.

Miss Hannigan tried to hide her disdain. "Oh, that's Annie. She's been a very bad little girl."

"Is that so?" Grace winked at Annie. "Well, Miss Hannigan, as I was saying—"

"Look, I can explain." Miss Hannigan began, flustered. "It wasn't my fault. Annie escaped and—"

"Pardon me, Miss Hannigan, but I haven't the slightest idea what you're talking about. You see, I'm here on behalf of Mr. Oliver Warbucks."

Miss Hannigan had to sit down just from hearing his name mentioned. "Warbucks? Oliver Warbucks? *The* Oliver Warbucks?" Drops of sweat began to appear on Miss Hannigan's brow. Oliver Warbucks was the richest man in the world. He owned several homes, including one large mansion in Manhattan.

"That's right. I'm his private secretary. And as a gesture of charity, Mr. Warbucks has decided to invite one of the orphans to spend the Christmas holidays at his home. I've been sent here to select one for him."

Annie stood quietly in the corner, listening. An orphan at Warbucks mansion—it was almost too good to be true!

"He wants one of the orphans for Christmas?" Miss Hannigan asked, dumbfounded.

"Yes, Miss Hannigan."

"Well, what sort of orphan's he lookin' for?"

"I suppose she should be friendly," Grace began. "And smart." She locked eyes with Annie from across the room.

"The capital of Florida is Tallahassee!" Annie chimed.

"You be quiet!" ordered Miss Hannigan, pushing Annie aside. She turned to face Miss Farrell. "Yeah, what else?"

"Perhaps she could also be cheerful."

Annie broke out into hysterical laughter.

"That's enough outta you!" Miss Hannigan snapped. She stepped in front of Annie so she'd disappear from view. But Annie peeked out from behind and began tugging at a tendril of her curly red hair.

"Oh, and one last thing, Miss Hannigan. Mr. Warbucks prefers redheaded children. Yes. That's right," Grace said.

"You sure? Red hair? I'm afraid we ain't got any redheaded orphans around here. Nope." Miss Hannigan struggled to keep Annie still behind her.

"Well, what about this child here?" Grace gestured to Annie.

"Oh, boy!" Annie couldn't contain her excitement. Imagine, Christmas at Warbucks mansion!

"Oh, you wouldn't want Annie. She's a load of trouble. Big liar. Huge," Miss Hannigan prattled on.

"Somehow I doubt that, Miss Hannigan." Grace crouched down low to meet Annie's eyes from behind Miss Hannigan's knobby legs. "What do you say, Annie? Would you like to spend two weeks at Mr. Warbucks's home for Christmas?"

"Gee, would I!" Annie exclaimed. What a treat! After all her rotten luck, Annie would never have dreamed of something like this. *Wait until the girls hear!* she thought.

"Now hold on just a second," Miss Hannigan interjected. "You can have any orphan in the orphanage except Annie."

"But why not?" Miss Farrell frowned.

"Like I told ya, she's trouble!"

Miss Farrell cleared her throat with authority. "If this has anything to do with what you described earlier, about Annie's escape, I would be happy to call up the Board of Orphans and explain. . . ."

Miss Hannigan piped up. "No, no, no. That

won't be necessary." She giggled nervously. "If it's Annie you want, it's Annie you get."

"Well, it's Annie I want," Miss Farrell proclaimed. "And I'll need you to sign this temporary release form, giving Annie permission to be absent from the orphanage for two weeks under the supervision of Mr. Warbucks." Miss Farrell set her leather briefcase down on Miss Hannigan's desk and pulled out a crisp piece of paper with teeny-tiny lettering. She placed it face-up on the table where Miss Hannigan sat. "Sign it," she ordered.

"Yeah, I'll sign it," Miss Hannigan grumbled.

When she was done, Grace slipped the paper back into her briefcase. "Well, Annie. We should be on our way. Why don't you get your coat—"

"Coat?" interrupted Miss Hannigan. "She ain't got no coat."

Miss Farrell glowered at Miss Hannigan sulking at her desk, then turned to Annie and smiled cheerfully. "Then we'll have to stop at Bergdorf Goodman on the way and pick out a nice warm winter coat. What do you say, Annie?"

"Oh, boy!" Annie shook with glee. Then she remembered her friends, whom she hadn't seen for months. "Gee, Miss Farrell, would you mind if I said hello and good-bye to my friends first? Ya know, before we leave?"

"Of course, Annie. I'll just tell the driver we'll be another minute or so."

Annie looked confused. "Driver?"

"Yes, dear. Mr. Warbucks's limousine is outside waiting for us," Miss Farrell explained matter-of-factly.

"Wow! Me, in a limousine? I can hardly believe it!"

Miss Farrell grinned at Annie's excitement. "I'll just wait up here while you say your good-byes."

Annie crept down the stairs to the basement. The girls were scrubbing the floors on their hands and knees. Miss Hannigan never let them rest for one second.

"It's a hard-knock life," Pepper complained. "All we do is work, day and night."

"You got that right," said Kate.

"I miss Annie," Molly moaned. "When's she comin' home?"

"For the hundredth time, Molly. Annie ain't comin' home," Pepper said, annoyed.

Molly sniffled, holding back tears.

Pepper rolled her eyes, "Aw, not again!"

"Hey, Pepper. Why don't ya leave her alone, huh?" Annie's voice came from the bottom of the stairs.

"Annie!" Molly shrieked. She ran to Annie and nearly knocked her over with a great big hug. "You're back! I told them. I said you'd come home."

"Well, yes. I'm sort of back," said Annie.

"What happened, the cops get ya?" Pepper teased.

"Shh!" Annie whispered. She didn't want Miss Farrell to change her mind about taking Annie for Christmas. "Yes, but now some nice lady is taking me to live in a big ol' mansion for two weeks!"

Molly's lips quivered. No Annie for another two weeks?

"Don't worry, Molly." Annie pulled her into a hug. "I'll be back real soon to take care of you like I used to. I promise."

The girls followed Annie up the stairs. They ran to the front windows of the orphanage and put their noses up against the glass to see the huge limousine parked on the street outside.

"Whoa, Annie!" Pepper exclaimed.

"Are you ready to go, Annie?" Miss Farrell came up behind her and placed a hand on each shoulder.

"Ready!" Annie practically yelled. She hugged everyone good-bye, and then let Miss Farrell usher her out the door.

"Good riddance," Miss Hannigan droned from her office desk.

The girls waved from the windows, shouting, "Merry Christmas, Annie!"

Annie waved back, shrugging her shoulders. She had no idea what the next two weeks would bring, but she was excited to find out.

Chapter Four

Miss Farrell escorted Annie to the jet-black limousine. A chauffeur dressed in an elegant suit opened the door for them.

Annie sank down into the seat. She had never felt anything so comfortable before! The plush cushions were soft enough to sleep on, and the heat made the inside of the car cozy and warm.

The chauffeur took his place in the front seat of the car and shut the door. "To Bergdorf's, please," Miss Farrell said. And off they went.

They drove up Fifth Avenue. Though Annie had lived in New York her entire life, this was a part of Manhattan she'd never seen before. Glamorous shops with expensive clothing displayed in windows, old churches with stone steps, and exclusive restaurants lined the streets.

The car stopped in front of a beautiful department store. Miss Farrell led Annie inside. It was overwhelming. All around her were racks and tables of luxurious clothing and accessories.

After looking around for a little while, Miss Farrell picked out a pink wool coat with a fur collar for Annie and a matching hat. Annie tried them on and spun around in front of the mirror. She'd never been pampered like this, but she liked it. Without even checking the price tags, Miss Farrell brought the coat and hat up to the salesclerk. "Charge these to Mr. Warbucks's account, please."

Miss Farrell slipped the coat back onto Annie's shoulders and placed the hat atop her head. Then she clasped Annie's hand and they walked out of the store and back to the limousine. "To the Warbucks mansion," Miss Farrell instructed the driver as they got in.

The only home Annie had ever known was the orphanage. So when she stepped out of the limousine in front of a six-story, marble-pillared mansion, her jaw nearly dropped. "Mr. Warbucks lives here all by himself?" asked Annie uncertainly.

"Oh, goodness no, dear," Miss Farrell explained, smiling. "We all live here. Mr. Warbucks has full-time staff accommodations."

"So you live here, too?"

"That's right," Miss Farrell said. She took

Annie's hand, and they walked up to the large front door together. She knocked twice, and almost instantly, the door opened. A tall gentleman in a green uniform stood at attention beside it.

"Annie, this is Drake, Mr. Warbucks's butler."

"Hi, there!" Annie said, sticking out her hand to shake his.

Drake looked confused. He was a serious man and wasn't used to making the acquaintance of little girls. With some hesitation, he held out his hand, and Annie shook it hard.

"Pleased to meet ya," Annie said brightly.

When Annie finally took her first step into the foyer, she couldn't believe her eyes. It was like being in a museum. Never before had she seen such high ceilings, except perhaps at Grand Central Terminal. But that was a train station, and this was someone's house! Annie couldn't hide her amazement. "You sure you live here?"

she asked. It was simply too hard to imagine anyone living in such a grand home.

Miss Farrell laughed. "Yes, Annie. And for the next two weeks, it will be your home, too. Now come along. I'd like to introduce you to the rest of Mr. Warbucks's staff."

Annie began to follow, and Drake walked alongside her.

"May I take your coat and hat, miss?" he asked.

Annie looked unsure. "Will I get 'em back?"

Miss Farrell chuckled. "Of course, dear."

Annie felt embarrassed for asking, but she'd never owned such nice things before.

She shrugged off her coat, took the hat from her head, and handed them to Drake, who bowed stiffly before turning away.

Annie and Miss Farrell stood in the empty foyer for a moment, but they were soon greeted by dozens of men and women in black-and-white uniforms. They stood in formation on the grand staircase, women in front, men behind.

Miss Farrell piped up. "Everyone, this is Annie. She will be staying with us for the next two weeks and joining us for the Christmas holiday."

"Miss," the group chorused, bowing and curtsying.

"Hi, everyone." Annie waved.

"Now, Annie. What would you like to do first? You can do anything you'd like."

Annie thought for a moment. She looked around the large room: the floor-to-ceiling windows, the glossy marble floors. Then she turned back to Miss Farrell. "Well, I can start on the floors. I can give them a good scrub. Then the windows, I guess."

Polite laughter came from the staff, and Miss Farrell covered her mouth as a small giggle escaped. "Oh, Annie. You won't need to lift a finger while you're here."

"I won't?" Annie had assumed she'd been taken to the mansion to help prepare for the holidays.

"Goodness, no. You're our guest! And we're here to attend to your every need. Your only task is to have a swell time."

Annie grinned from ear to ear. "Oh, boy!"

"Mrs. Pugh will serve you breakfast in bed every morning. And Annette will make up your bed and tidy your room."

"I have a room? All to myself?" Annie and all the other girls shared a room at the orphanage, and there was never any privacy.

"Well, of course. Now let me see. . . . Ah, yes, the swimming pool is in the rear."

"A pool? *Inside* the house?"

Miss Farrell nodded.

"I think I'm gonna like it here." Annie grinned.

Chapter Five

"**N**ow, Annie," Miss Farrell said after dismissing the staff, "I'll show you to your room so you can settle in before Mr. Warbucks arrives."

Annie took Miss Farrell's hand, and up the staircase they went, stepping into a hallway lined with plush white carpeting. Annie's was the first room on the left.

"Here we are," Miss Farrell began, opening the bedroom door. "This is where you'll be staying while you're here. I hope it's to your liking."

Annie was speechless for the first time in her life. The room was larger than the bedroom at the orphanage times ten. Polished wood furniture sat in different corners, and a large bed covered in fine silk linens and topped with fluffy pillows was at the center. "All this for me?" Annie finally asked.

"All for you," Miss Farrell replied. "I'll just let you get comfortable. Dinner will be served shortly, and Drake will be up to escort you down to the dining room."

Miss Farrell walked out and closed the door behind her.

"Gee, this is the life," Annie said to herself as she rolled onto the soft bed. For a moment, she thought what it would be like to live with a proper family in a real home. With a mom and dad, and maybe even a little brother or sister to boss around. *Must be nice,* Annie thought.

She got up to take a tour of the room. One door led to a huge walk-in closet that was large enough to be another bedroom. Inside, the racks were filled with beautiful clothing in all sizes. Another door opened into what turned out to be a large bathroom with a claw-foot porcelain tub, and little rose-colored soaps. Fresh flowers bloomed in a vase on the countertop. Annie put her nose up to them and breathed in. Then she lifted up her own arm and took a whiff. She wrinkled her nose. "Better get cleaned up before dinner."

After soaking in a warm, bubbly bath for close to half an hour, Annie wrapped herself in a soft towel and chose one of the dresses hanging in the closet. It was a dark green velvet frock with a white collar. Annie almost felt foolish wearing it, after years of the same old threadbare sweater. But now she looked like she belonged in a lavish mansion on the Upper East Side.

Annie was sitting on the bed awaiting Drake's

arrival when she heard a booming voice from down below.

"Hello! I'm home!"

Annie crept to the bedroom door and opened it carefully so as not to make a sound.

"Welcome home, Mr. Warbucks," she heard Drake say.

"Good to be home." The voice spoke again. Then without missing a beat: "Grace! My messages!"

"Yes, Mr. Warbucks. President Roosevelt called from the White House. He says he wishes to speak with you immediately," Grace announced.

"I'll call him back tomorrow," Mr. Warbucks stated. "Who else?"

The sound of flipping pages could be heard—Miss Farrell skimming through her notebook. "John D. Rockefeller, Albert Einstein, and Mahatma Gandhi, sir."

"Nothing important, then."

Annie tiptoed out of her room and peered over the banister into the foyer where Mr. Warbucks stood surrounded by his staff.

"Drake, I'll be working for the rest of the night in my study. Please have my dinner brought to me there. And Grace, I'll need you to assist me. There's much work to be done."

Annie peered down from the top of the staircase. She held on to the railing and stepped down one foot at a time. Miss Farrell noticed her coming and met Annie halfway, escorting her down the rest of the stairs and up to where Mr. Warbucks stood like a large statue.

"Mr. Warbucks, I want to introduce you to Annie, the orphan who will be staying with us for Christmas."

Mr. Warbucks turned. He was a large man with a shiny bald head and piercing blue eyes. He towered over Annie and looked down at her round, freckled face. "Who?"

"Annie, sir. Your publicist suggested you

invite an orphan here for Christmas to improve your image, and at your request, I selected one for you."

"Aren't orphans supposed to be boys? Like Oliver Twist?"

"Well, I suppose some of them are boys. But you never specified—"

Seeing Annie standing there in her dress, Mr. Warbucks quickly changed the subject. "That's okay. . . . We're delighted to have you for Christmas, Annie." Mr. Warbucks stepped behind Annie, placing a hand on her shoulder. "What are we supposed to do with this child for two weeks?" he mouthed to Miss Farrell over Annie's head.

Miss Farrell shrugged. Then an idea came to mind. "How would you like to go to a movie, Annie?"

"Yes, a fine idea, Grace," said Mr. Warbucks. "How 'bout it, Annie?"

"I've never been to a movie before." Annie's eyes lit up.

"Never been to a movie?" Mr. Warbucks said, shocked. "We'll have to fix that right away. You'll go to the Roxy—nothing but the best for you, Annie."

"Oh, boy!" Annie cried.

"Grace—after the movie I want you to take Annie to Rumplemayer's for an ice cream soda, then for a carriage ride across Central Park—"

"Aren't you coming with us?" Annie asked.

"Sorry, Annie," Mr. Warbucks said matter-of-factly. "There's far too much work to be done. You see, I've just returned from a trip to visit my factories and—"

"Aw, gee . . ." Annie slumped her shoulders.

"Yes, what is it?" Mr. Warbucks said, impatient.

"I guess I just thought . . . well . . ."

"Yes, yes?"

"Since it's my first night and all, do you think you could take me?"

"W-well . . . I . . . you see—"

"Aw, gee . . ." Annie repeated.

Mr. Warbucks gazed down at Annie's angelic-looking face. He looked up at Miss Farrell, who only grinned at him, awaiting his reply.

"Drake!" Mr. Warbucks called rather loudly.

The butler seemed to appear in no time at all. "Yes, Mr. Warbucks?"

"Coats! For Miss Farrell, Miss Annie, and me."

"Yes, sir." Drake bowed his head and turned on his heel to fetch their things.

"I'm taking the night off," Mr. Warbucks said. "We're going to the movies."

Chapter Six

Mr. Warbucks insisted they walk to the Roxy. Annie was toasty warm in her new coat and hat, and happy as could be flanked on either side by Miss Farrell and Mr. Warbucks—two of the nicest people she'd ever met.

It was a night Annie wouldn't soon forget. First they saw a film at the Roxy, an upscale movie theater, where Mr. Warbucks bought her popcorn and candy. Then afterward, Mr. Warbucks treated Annie to a gigantic chocolate ice cream soda at Rumplemayer's, the famous restaurant on Central Park South. The frothy drink was so big, Annie couldn't finish it all, but Mr. Warbucks helped out as best he could. Then the three of them took a horse-and-carriage ride through Central Park. The air was crisp and chilly, but Annie wouldn't have changed a thing. For the first time in maybe forever, she felt loved.

By the end of the night, Annie was exhausted. Miss Farrell had the limousine come to take them home, and a sleeping Annie nestled herself close to Mr. Warbucks in the backseat. At this, Mr. Warbucks shifted his body to wiggle her off. But seeing Miss Farrell's expression from across the car forced him to soften, and he let Annie rest on him until they made it home.

Once they arrived in front of the mansion, the chauffeur got out and promptly opened their doors. Mr. Warbucks was trapped under Annie's sleeping body. Shrugging his shoulders, he looked to Miss Farrell for help. She motioned for Mr. Warbucks to carry Annie inside and up to her bedroom.

"Carry her?" he whispered.

"She looks so peaceful," Miss Farrell said. "It would be a shame to wake her now."

And so Mr. Warbucks held Annie like a baby and carried her up the walkway, into the foyer, and up the stairs, before laying her gently on her soft, king-size bed.

For a moment, Annie's eyes fluttered open. It took a second for her to realize where she was, but then she saw Mr. Warbucks's silhouette in the dark.

Before he could leave, Annie said, "Thanks for everything, Mr. Warbucks. I had a swell time, I really did."

"I'm glad, Annie." He paused. "And I'd be lying if I said I didn't have a swell time, too."

With that, he left the room and closed the door quietly. Annie smiled and laid her head back down on the pillow, drifting off to sleep.

Mr. Warbucks might not have realized it yet, but the young orphan had found her way into his heart.

The next few days were better than Annie had ever expected. Miss Farrell took her to the indoor pool, and even had an instructor teach her how to swim. She took tennis lessons, but it turned out she wasn't quite a natural with a racket. The tennis pro came away with bruises from being struck so many times with tennis balls.

But even though Annie was able to do things she had never even dreamed of before, she missed spending time with Mr. Warbucks. He was almost always hidden away in his study, making important phone calls and doing something called "paperwork."

One morning, Annie found Mr. Warbucks having breakfast at the head of the long dining-room table. He had a newspaper open with his head hidden behind the large pages.

Annie snuck up next to him. "Wha'cha doin', Mr. Warbucks?"

Mr. Warbucks jumped and nearly fell over in his chair. His legs hit the underside of the table, shaking all the glassware. Coffee splashed out of his cup and splattered on the tabletop.

"Annie!" he began, righting himself. "Didn't see you there."

"That's okay," she said. "Reading anything good?"

"Ahh," he uttered. "Business is bad. But I suppose that isn't news anymore."

Annie nodded like she understood, but really the only business she'd ever been in was selling apples.

"You see, Annie, I've worked my whole life for this," he said, gesturing to their grand surroundings.

"Uh huh."

"Never took a day off in my life. No vacations or holidays. It's been all work all the time."

Annie could relate to that. She'd been doing manual labor at the orphanage since the time she could walk.

"But you know what?" he said, slamming his fist on the table. "It's time I put my work to rest for a change. My businesses can take care of themselves. Annie, I'm going to show you New York like you've never seen it before. What do you say?"

"Oh, boy, oh, boy!" Annie cried, and hopped up and down on her toes.

"Draaaake!" Mr. Warbucks's voice echoed across the dining room.

Drake appeared in an instant. "Sir?"

"Bring the Rolls Royce around," Mr. Warbucks ordered. "We're taking a tour of the city, Annie and I."

"Right away, sir." Drake disappeared almost as quickly.

Mr. Warbucks showed Annie the Stock Exchange and the Statue of Liberty. They took the Staten Island ferry and rode bicycles through Central Park. They ate lunch at the Waldorf Astoria. Then Mr. Warbucks took her to the top of the Empire State Building, and they saw the Rockettes perform at Radio City Music Hall.

The next day, Mr. Warbucks rented an airplane for a few hours and flew Annie over New York City. He pointed out all the landmarks and some of the tallest buildings in the world.

"To think I've lived here all my life and never knew about any of these places!" Annie said over the noise, smiling so hard her cheeks hurt.

But it was more than just these new experiences that explained Annie's happiness. Mr. Warbucks had become her very best friend, and she enjoyed spending time with him.

The truth of it was, Mr. Warbucks enjoyed Annie's company as well. In fact, he couldn't bear to send her back to the orphanage after Christmas was over. He made up his mind to do something completely out of character.

Late at night, after Annie had gone to bed, Mr. Warbucks called Miss Farrell into his office.

"Yes, Mr. Warbucks?" she said quietly.

"Grace, I've uh . . ." He shuffled the papers on his desk and stood up from his office chair. "I've decided to adopt Annie," he said with some embarrassment.

"Oh, Mr. Warbucks, how wonderful!"

But Mr. Warbucks wouldn't allow himself to get sentimental. "Contact my attorney and have him draw up the adoption papers," he demanded.

"Of course, sir. Is there anything else?" Miss Farrell asked, as she finished jotting down the orders.

"Actually, yes," Mr. Warbucks said. "Tomorrow morning, run over to Tiffany's and pick up a silver locket. Have it engraved with an *A* for *Annie*."

Miss Farrell couldn't hide her enthusiasm. She'd become fond of the little orphan girl herself and warmed at the thought of having Annie stay with them permanently.

"Absolutely, sir." She looked at Mr. Warbucks, expecting some sign of emotion.

Eventually, Mr. Warbucks caved, and his mouth formed a tight grin.

"That will be all, Grace. Good night."

"Good night, Mr. Warbucks." She stepped out and closed the door behind her.

Chapter Seven

Annie had been having such fun with Mr. Warbucks and Miss Farrell that she could hardly believe Christmas Day was right around the corner. After that, her visit to Warbucks mansion would be over, and she'd be forced to return to the orphanage. It would be good to see her friends again, but she couldn't deny how much she'd miss everyone. Most especially Mr. Warbucks.

Although Mr. Warbucks set aside his work

for Annie during the day, he couldn't neglect it entirely. At times, he could be seen in his office during the wee hours of the morning while Annie was still asleep and then late at night after Annie had gone to bed.

One night, though Annie tried and tried, she just couldn't get herself to fall asleep. So she trotted downstairs and spotted Mr. Warbucks pacing in his office.

Halfway down she realized she was still in her nightgown, but Mr. Warbucks wouldn't mind. The double doors of his office were open slightly, and Annie poked her rosy cheeks between them. "Work?" she guessed.

"Annie. You're up late," Mr. Warbucks said, but Annie could sense from his voice that something was wrong. "Come in."

"Is everything all right?" she asked.

"Actually, Annie, it's more than all right. Have a seat," he said. Annie sat in the leather chair by the desk, across from Mr. Warbucks.

"I'm glad you're here. The time has come for us to have a very serious discussion."

"This is about sendin' me back to the orphanage, isn't it?"

"Well . . . something like that. But Annie, what I'm trying to say, and this isn't easy for me, but—"

"That's okay, Mr. Warbucks. I understand. I'll go get my things." Annie pulled herself out of the chair and walked with her head down toward the door.

"What? Annie, where are you going?" Mr. Warbucks asked nervously.

"You've got work to do, and I'm just getting in the way."

Mr. Warbucks took three fast strides toward Annie and knelt down beside her so they were face-to-face. "No, Annie. What I'm trying to say is, I'd like to adopt you."

Annie gulped. "Adopt me?" Tears came to her eyes, and she forced them back.

"Yes, Annie." Mr. Warbucks clumsily pulled the pale-blue Tiffany box out of his jacket pocket and presented it to Annie. She opened it to find a shiny silver locket, an *A* engraved on the front. "It's a brand-new locket. I noticed that old, broken one you always wear and thought this could be the first gift from your ol' Daddy Warbucks." Mr. Warbucks, all smiles, waited patiently for Annie's response.

"That's really nice of you, Mr. Warbucks. And the locket, it's swell. But this old locket, it's from my real parents. And I just know they're out there somewhere. I've had it since I was a baby, and my parents have the other half. So when they come back for me, they'll know I'm their girl," Annie confessed.

The smile vanished from Mr. Warbucks's face. Not once had he imagined Annie refusing his offer. "I see," he said.

Annie could tell she'd upset him. Mr.

Warbucks had been nothing but nice to her, and now all she'd done was disappoint him. But her whole life she'd been searching for her parents, and she couldn't give up now.

"I really do love the locket," she said.

Mr. Warbucks smiled sadly. "Consider it an early Christmas present," he said. He stood up and patted Annie on the head.

Annie gave him a quick hug and then raced up the stairs and into her room. She carefully placed the box with the locket inside the top drawer of her dresser. It was a beautiful necklace, but Annie couldn't bear to replace her old one. Not when she still had hope that her parents were out there somewhere.

Chapter Eight

For the first time in his life, Mr. Warbucks couldn't argue to get his way. Nor could he buy himself what he wanted. Annie had made herself very clear—finding her parents was the most important thing. And though it hurt Mr. Warbucks to give her up, deep down all he really wanted was to make her happy. If that meant bringing her parents to her, then, by gosh, he would do everything in his power to make that happen.

The following morning, Mr. Warbucks placed calls to the FBI and President Roosevelt to begin a search for Annie's parents. He even offered a reward for anyone who had information on their whereabouts.

Annie awoke to the sound of many voices and heels clicking on the marble floor of the foyer. She jumped out of bed, ran out into the hall, and leaned over the banister. Every one of Mr. Warbucks's staff members hurried about.

What's going on? she wondered. Quickly, she made her way downstairs and into Mr. Warbucks's office. He had a telephone held up to each ear and was speaking into each of them. "Now, you listen to me. I want them found, and I want them found today. Do you hear me?" Then on the other line, "Yes, that's right. Fifty-thousand-dollar reward." Annie didn't have a clue what was going on, but soon enough Mr. Warbucks hung up both telephones and was ready to explain.

"If your parents are out there, Annie, then we're going to find them. I've got my top men on the case. And if I'm not mistaken, the entire country will be informed of your missing parents by tomorrow evening."

Annie's eyes went wide. If anyone could find her parents, it was Mr. Warbucks. Finally, she'd get to meet her mom and dad! "What about the locket? Did you tell them about the locket?"

"That's between you and me, Annie. If a couple comes forward knowing everything about you *and* they have the other half of the locket, then we'll know it's really your mother and father."

"Oh, I get it. That way we won't be fooled by any fakers claiming to be my folks."

"Right you are, Annie," Mr. Warbucks said.

After so much waiting, it was difficult for Annie to contain her excitement at the thought of meeting the parents she'd never known. Mr. Warbucks thought of an idea. "Well, Annie, we've got everyone working around the clock to find your parents. What say you and I take a little trip."

"A trip, Mr. Warbucks?"

"It's high time I visit the president. He's been hounding me for weeks now."

"President Roosevelt?" Annie asked in shock.

"Yes, that president," Mr. Warbucks said. He wasn't very happy to be leaving home to talk politics, but it was all he could do to take Annie's mind off the search for her parents.

They were driven to Pennsylvania Station in midtown, where they boarded a train to Washington, D.C. Mr. Warbucks had his own private railway car. The ride would take several hours, so Annie and Mr. Warbucks had plenty of time to talk.

"What do you think, Mr. Warbucks? Do you think my parents are out there?"

"I'm not sure, Annie. But if they are, my guess is they'll show up at my doorstep by the time we arrive home."

"Gee, you really think so?"

"We'll just have to see," Mr. Warbucks said kindly. In truth, Mr. Warbucks had his doubts. If Annie's parents were out there, surely they would have come for her well before now. But there was always hope. And Annie had enough of that to spread around for days.

When they arrived in Washington, they were picked up by a limousine with the presidential seal on the door and little American flags on either side of the front. Not five minutes passed before they pulled up in front of the White House.

"Golly!" Annie sighed. "Would you look at that?"

If Annie was impressed by Mr. Warbucks's Manhattan mansion, she was absolutely floored by the president's home. The huge White House sat on acres upon acres of perfectly manicured lawn, and a high metal fence went all the way around the property.

Annie and Mr. Warbucks were escorted onto the grounds by one of the guards and shown into the Oval Office. President Roosevelt sat at the head of a large table with the members of his cabinet.

"Ah, Oliver. So glad you could come," President Roosevelt said when they entered the room. "And whom do we have here?" he asked, noticing Annie ducking behind Mr. Warbucks's leg.

"This is my good friend Annie. I couldn't resist bringing her with me. She wanted to meet you."

Annie slowly came forward to shake the man's hand. "It's a pleasure to meet you, Mr. President," she said with confidence.

"And you!" he replied.

One of the men seated at the table spoke up. "All right, Mr. President. It's time to discuss more important matters."

Mr. Warbucks turned to Annie. "Annie, why don't you wait for me outside."

"Nonsense!" the president said. "Annie can stay. In fact, with a child in the room, we'll all be on our best behavior." He winked at Annie and she winked back.

They all took their seats at the table. The group began talking about the poor state of the country. How millions of men and women were out of work and people were starving on the streets. Annie knew all about it from her days at the shantytown but decided to stay silent. Each person had different ideas on how to make things better, but they couldn't agree on anything. Eventually, they began to argue.

"The sun'll come out tomorrow," Annie said softly. "Bet your bottom dollar that tomorrow there'll be sun."

President Roosevelt did his best to quiet the group. "What did you say, child?"

Now all eyes were on Annie. Suddenly, she didn't feel so confident anymore. But she urged herself to continue. "Well, I just think, if we spent more time thinkin' about the good things that might be comin' tomorrow instead of the bad things that are happenin' today, you might get started on makin' those good things happen."

"Now, that's interesting," the president said, rubbing his chin. "Tomorrow, huh?"

"Tomorrow," Annie repeated.

"Tomorrow!" the group cheered. Suddenly, everyone was feeling more optimistic, and it was all because of Annie.

At that moment, a White House guard entered the room to make an announcement. "Excuse me," he said. "I don't mean to interrupt, but a telegram has just come in for you, Mr. Warbucks, from your secretary in New York. She says there are hundreds of couples crowding the street outside your home, all of them claiming to be Annie's parents. She's begun screening them, but she suggests you come home at once."

"Well, I'll be darned," said Mr. Warbucks.

"Did you hear, Mr. Warbucks—hundreds of couples! One of them has to be my real mom and dad," Annie assumed.

Mr. Warbucks nodded solemnly. If one of the couples did turn out to be Annie's parents, that meant his time with Annie would come to an end rather quickly, and Mr. Warbucks wasn't quite prepared for that.

President Roosevelt was the first to speak up. "Well, Oliver, it looks like you have important business to attend to at home. Though I've enjoyed your company, and yours, too, Annie, I suspect you should be getting back to New York immediately."

"Yes, Mr. President. I believe we will," Mr.

Warbucks responded. "Come along, Annie."

"It was nice meeting you, Mr. President." Annie curtsied.

"And even nicer meeting you, Annie. I think we've all learned a little something from you today." He cleared his throat and yelled, "The sun'll come out tomorrow!"

Chapter Nine

When Annie and Mr. Warbucks arrived home, the crowd of couples had completely gone. "Maybe that means Miss Farrell found my folks! They could be waiting inside for me right now!" Annie ran ahead of Mr. Warbucks up the walkway and into the foyer, where she found Miss Farrell standing to greet them.

"Have you found them? Are they here?" Annie asked eagerly.

Miss Farrell frowned gently and breathed a

heavy sigh. "I'm sorry to have to tell you this, Annie. But out of all the couples I screened, none of them, not one, knew about the locket."

Annie was crestfallen. All those people were impostors looking for reward money. None of them were there for her, or even cared.

Mr. Warbucks soon caught up with Annie. When he entered the foyer, he glanced up at Miss Farrell for an answer, but she simply shook her head. As much as Mr. Warbucks wanted Annie for himself, he had never wished for any of this to happen. He only wanted her to be happy, and he'd done everything he could to make it so.

But if her parents hadn't been located after all their searching, it was likely they weren't out there at all. The problem was breaking the news to Annie.

Annie spent the rest of Christmas Eve up in her room, alone. She was devastated. Was it possible that after all this time, her parents would never come for her? For twelve years, she'd hoped and dreamed the day would come when she'd reunite with her mother and father. Now it looked like that day was never going to come. She'd be an orphan forever.

Then she remembered the locket. Not the old one from her parents, but the new one from Mr. Warbucks. Hadn't he been as good as a father to her these last two weeks? Hadn't Miss Farrell doted on her and made her feel loved? What Annie had always wanted was right here.

Annie went over to the dresser drawer where she had hidden the tiny blue box. She opened it and took out the locket. Finally, she was ready to put the past behind her and start a new life with Mr. Warbucks. Carefully she unclasped her old locket and placed it on the dresser. Then she picked up the new Tiffany necklace and slipped it over her head. The locket slid down under her shirt. *Tomorrow morning,* Annie thought, *I'll tell Mr. Warbucks that I want him to adopt me. Tomorrow morning, I'll finally have a family to call my own.*

Annie fell asleep that night without any trouble at all. But when she awoke the next morning, she was filled with jitters of excitement. After her bath, one of the maids came to style her hair and help her into the dress Mr. Warbucks had bought especially for her to wear on Christmas Day. It was made of red velvet and had a white collar and white cuffs.

After all the primping was done, Annie walked down the grand staircase and stopped in her tracks. She couldn't believe what she was seeing. Downstairs in the foyer was the largest Christmas tree Annie had ever laid eyes on. It was covered from top to bottom in shiny red and green ornaments and had gold tinsel wrapped around it. A spectacular crystal star stood at the top, sparkling brightly. Underneath the tree were about a hundred wrapped boxes, with different colored ribbons. It was a sight to behold. Annie ran down the rest of the stairs and found Mr. Warbucks sitting in his office.

"Merry Christmas, Annie! Don't you look swell." He grinned. He was happy to see her glowing as brightly as the star on the tree.

"Merry Christmas, Mr. Warbucks." She approached him.

"Come in," he said.

Annie walked over and he patted his lap. He lifted her onto his leg. "Annie, I'm sorry we couldn't find your parents," he said sadly.

"That's okay, Mr. Warbucks. I know you tried your best. Maybe they just don't want me anymore," she decided.

"Well, Annie, that's not exactly the case. You

see, I received a phone call last night from the FBI. They think they know what happened to your mom and dad. They have it on record that your parents—well—long ago, they . . ."

"You don't have to explain, Mr. Warbucks. I understand. Anyway, I've thought about it. And there's something I want to tell you."

Mr. Warbucks looked curious. "Yes, Annie. What is it?"

"I've been thinking about that locket you gave me. And well, I have all the family I need right here. And if it's all right, I mean, if you'll still have me, I'd love for you to be my Daddy Warbucks."

Mr. Warbucks was astonished. This wasn't what he was expecting!

"Mr. Warbucks?" Annie prodded, hoping he hadn't changed his mind.

"Of course, Annie," he said, smiling broadly. "It would be my greatest honor." They embraced and then Annie pulled the locket from under her dress collar, holding it out for him to see.

"My first Christmas present from Daddy Warbucks," she said.

Later on, Annie sat with Daddy Warbucks and Miss Farrell by the fireplace, listening to Christmas carols on the radio.

"Oh, Annie," Daddy Warbucks began. "I have another gift for you."

"More gifts?" Annie questioned. Already she'd received the locket, plus a number of other treats, including chocolates from Rumplemayer's, a pink cashmere scarf to match her coat and hat, and a new pair of leather shoes.

"I couldn't resist," he said. At that moment, the doorbell rang. Drake went to answer it, and in poured all Annie's friends from the orphanage, trailed by a disheveled-looking Miss Hannigan.

"Merry Christmas, Annie!" the girls all said at once. Annie hugged her pals.

She took the girls on a tour of the house, and then they each got some of the presents from under the tree. After that, everyone gathered together in the dining room, feasting on roast turkey, mashed potatoes, and biscuits and gravy to their hearts' content.

"I can't believe you're gonna live here, Annie!" Pepper exclaimed.

"Yeah, Annie. This place is like a castle!" said Molly.

"Mr. Warbucks says you can come visit me anytime. Every week, if you want," Annie said.

Just then, Mr. Warbucks came into the dining room, holding a large red box.

"Another gift?" Annie asked in disbelief.

"Last one, Annie. I promise," said Mr. Warbucks with a smile. He set the box down next to Annie's chair.

Tentatively, Annie lifted the lid off the box. Before she could pull it off all the way, it sprang open, and an enormous, hairy body flung itself at her. "Sandy!" Annie shrieked.

Daddy Warbucks winked. "Merry Christmas, Annie."

Annie smiled. It was a merry Christmas indeed!